# Love Beyond Boundaries

1. **Hidden Truths**
   - Thomas and Jasmin's early lives in different families and cultures.
   - Their internal struggles with gender identity.
   - Their experiences growing up—Thomas in a conservative Christian family, Jasmin in a traditional Indian-American household.
2. **Breaking free**
   - **Thomas's Journey to Arora**
   - Hiding his true identity from his deeply religious parents.
   - Moving out at 18, finding a job, and transitioning into Arora.
   - Facing rejection from his parents and struggling to build a new life.
   - Overcoming workplace and social discrimination, becoming a successful corporate lawyer.

- **Jasmin's Journey to Ryan**
- Struggles with gender identity in school, facing bullying and misunderstanding.
- Turning 18, gaining the freedom to transition into Ryan.
- Initial disappointment from parents but later acceptance and love.
- Pursuing his passion for business, starting his own company.

3. **A Fateful Encounter**
    - Arora and Ryan randomly meet at a coffee shop in New York.
    - A subtle connection, a "love wave."
    - Their initial conversation and mysterious attraction.

4. **Unraveling Bonds**
    - Ryan's startup requires legal counsel, and Arora's firm is assigned to the case.
    - Their professional and personal worlds collide.
    - Slowly bonding over work meetings, lunch outings, and shared experiences.

5. **Falling in Love**
    - Opening up about their past struggles.
    - Sharing stories of rejection, acceptance, and transformation.
    - Comforting each other and realizing they are meant for one another.

6. **Challenges and Drama**
    - Facing workplace discrimination and past bullies reappearing.
    - Ryan's parents embracing Arora, but Arora's parents refusing to accept her.
    - A legal battle where Arora has to defend Ryan's company, strengthening their bond.

7. **Happy Ending**
    - Overcoming obstacles together, proving love transcends all boundaries.
    - Arora's parents slowly coming to terms with their daughter's happiness.
    - Ryan and Arora solidifying their love and planning a future together.
    - A heartwarming ending showcasing their strength and unbreakable bond.

# Chapter 1: Hidden Truths

Thomas grew up in a quiet suburban neighborhood in New York, where every lawn was trimmed to perfection and every Sunday was sacred. In his home, religion wasn't just a belief—it was the air they breathed. His father, Deacon Harold Whitmore, preached with a voice that could silence a crowd, and his mother, Eleanor, led the choir with a smile that masked judgment. Their world was orderly, unquestionable, and built on the idea that God's design was infallible.

But Thomas knew—had always known—that something inside him didn't align with their divine order.

From the time he was six, he'd sneak into his sister's room to run his fingers over her lace dresses, fascinated not by their beauty, but by how they made him feel. At ten, he cried himself to sleep after being caught by his father trying on his mother's pearl earrings.

“What are you, a girl?” his father had growled, yanking them off his ears. “Don’t ever disgrace this family like that again.”

That night, Thomas learned two things: how to lie, and how to bury his truth so deep no one could find it.

At school, he played the part with painful precision.

The hallways of St. Michael's were a battleground. Each day, Thomas donned his armor: the letterman jacket, the practiced swagger, the carefully constructed jokes. He pitched fastballs, cracked crude jokes in the locker room, and flirted with Madison Greene just enough to convince everyone—including himself—that maybe he could pretend forever.

But the locker room was a minefield. The other boys, emboldened by the pack, would slap his back a little too hard, their eyes lingering a little too long when he changed. He'd force a laugh, flexing his arm, trying to project an image of carefree masculinity. But inside, he felt like he was disappearing.

In class, he'd sit ramrod straight, mind a million miles away, sketching dresses in the margins of his notebooks. The teachers' words would wash over him, replaced in his mind by images of flowing chiffon and shimmering sequins.

Even Madison, with her bright smile and easy laughter, was a part of the performance. When he walked her home from school, his hand brushing hers, he felt a strange disconnect. He was playing a role, and she was the unwitting audience.

Pretending was a prison. Each laugh he forced, each masculine stride he faked, pushed him further from the person he longed to be.

The school's annual talent show was a particular torment. He wanted to design costumes, to help the girls shine on stage, but he knew his father would be in the audience. The thought of being seen in that light, of confirming his deepest fear, kept his hands tied. He sang in the choir instead, his voice strong but his spirit muted.

When he was alone, though—when the house was quiet and the world stopped demanding—he'd lock his bedroom door, pull out his sketchpad, and disappear into a world of chiffon, velvet, and satin. He drew gowns that whispered freedom, heels that shouted defiance, and wigs that promised authenticity. His dream? To walk down a street one day as her—Arora—not as a lie.

Meanwhile, across the city in a cluttered Queens apartment, Jasmin sat on her bed in a room painted pink against her will, glaring at her reflection. Her mother had just bought her a new lehenga for Diwali, complete with bangles and a matching bindi. It sat in the corner like a ghost, waiting to haunt her.

"Don't you love it, Baby?" her mom had beamed earlier, "You'll look like a princess!"

Jasmin had nodded, muttered thanks, and fought the urge to scream. Inside, she wasn't a princess. She wasn't anyone's daughter. The person she saw in her dreams wasn't wearing a dress—he was Ryan, sharp-jawed and strong, wearing a hoodie and jeans, arms wide open like wings.

At school, she tried blending in with the boys, but they saw her body first, not her mind.

The first time she'd tried out for the soccer team, the coach had stared at her, a strange mix of confusion and discomfort in his eyes. "You... you want to play *with the boys*?" he'd asked, as if she'd spoken in a foreign language. She'd nodded, her throat tight, but her gaze steady. She was fast, agile, a natural on the field. But they hadn't given her a chance.

In the hallways, the boys would jostle her, their laughter echoing, their words hitting like stones: "Tomboy." "Dyke." "Freak." She'd clench her fists, her heart a hard knot in her chest, and walk on.

When she spoke like them, they laughed. When she sat with them, they called her weird. The girls dismissed her too, whispering about how she “tried too hard” and “acted like a boy.” She didn’t fit anywhere.

Lunchtime was a daily tightrope walk. She'd sit at the edge of the cafeteria, a book propped up in front of her, trying to create a shield between herself and the world. But she could feel their eyes on her, the whispers that followed her like a shadow.

She took solace in long walks at night, hoodie up, binder strapped tight, headphones blasting Linkin Park or AR Rahman depending on her mood. In the shadows, she was Ryan. Not pretending—becoming.

She journaled furiously, pages filled with affirmations, sketches of masculine versions of herself, even a fake driver's license mock-up with the name "Ryan Patel." She wasn't just dreaming—she was preparing.

One night, during a particularly bad fight with her mother about wearing lipstick to a cousin's wedding, Jasmin locked herself in the bathroom, pressed her forehead against the mirror, and whispered, "Will they still love me if I tell them?"

The answer was a silence that echoed.

Thomas faced his own reckoning on a frigid December night. After dinner, he overheard his parents discussing a sermon series on "Gender Confusion." His father's voice boomed from the study: "It's a sickness, Eleanor. These kids need prayer, not affirmation. I won't have our son be one of them."

Thomas sat frozen on the stairs, tears dripping onto the polished wood floor.

That night, he didn't sleep. He stood in front of the mirror, holding one of his sketches—a flowing lavender dress with a slit and sequined shoulders—against his chest. In his mind, the reflection changed. The boy disappeared. Arora emerged.

"I see you," he whispered. "Even if no one else does."

As the months rolled by, the countdown to eighteen became a lifeline. A number carved into their hearts like a secret promise. Thomas saved every penny from his after-school job at the local bookstore. Jasmin collected tutorials on binding, packing, and voice training. Neither knew of the other's existence, but the universe already had plans. The same sky hung over them both, stars aligning quietly, patiently waiting for their moment to meet. Because hidden truths always demand to be known. And soon, theirs would no longer be hidden.

# Chapter 2: Breaking Free

The night Thomas turned eighteen, the Whitmore house was silent except for the ticking clock in the hallway. He stood by the window, backpack slung over his shoulder, heart pounding like a war drum. The letter he'd written to his parents sat on his neatly made bed, folded once, short and vague:

I'm sorry. I love you. But I have to live my truth. Please don't look for me. — Thomas

He opened the door with trembling hands and stepped into the cold January air. Snow flurried around him like whispers, like blessings. With one last look at the house where he'd buried himself for so long, he turned his back to it—finally free.

The bus to Manhattan smelled like diesel and stale fries. Thomas curled up in a seat by the window, forehead pressed to the glass, wondering if he'd made the biggest mistake of his life—or the bravest choice.

Manhattan was chaos. Crowded, loud, indifferent—perfect. No one knew him. No one stared. He was just another face in the crowd, and that anonymity was its own kind of salvation.

He found a tiny room in a crumbling building with water-stained ceilings and a lock that barely worked. The bed creaked like it was warning him not to get comfortable. But it was his space. For the first time, he wasn't under anyone's gaze.

To survive, he needed money, and quickly. He walked into countless businesses, his heart pounding with each application. Most places turned him away with a polite but firm, "We're not hiring," or a discomfort that spoke volumes. Finally, desperation led him to a 24-hour diner, its greasy windows promising a hot meal and, more importantly, a job.

He scrubbed dishes at the greasy diner where the manager yelled more than he spoke, and delivered takeout to high-rises where no one tipped. The work was grueling, the hours long, and the pay barely enough to cover rent and food. But it was a start.

Then, he saw the ad: "Night shift receptionist at The Grand Imperial Hotel." The idea of working in a place of such elegance, even in the dead of night, appealed to his sense of beauty and order. He applied, hoping his charm and quick learning would outweigh his lack of experience.

He got the job. The Grand Imperial Hotel was a world of polished marble, glittering chandeliers, and hushed elegance. At first, he was in awe. But the initial awe soon gave way to the reality of his situation.

The hotel staff, especially the night shift, was a mixed bag. Some were indifferent, focused on their tasks and eager to get through the night. Others were less accepting.

The bellman, a burly man named Tony, would make snide remarks, calling him "pretty boy" and questioning his ability to handle "real work." The night manager, Ms. Jenkins, was cold and demanding, assigning him the most unpleasant tasks, like cleaning up after rowdy guests or dealing with difficult deliveries.

"Don't expect any special treatment," she'd snap, her eyes devoid of warmth. "You're here to work, just like everyone else."

The loneliness was crushing. During his breaks, he'd retreat to the staff room, nursing a cup of instant coffee and sketching furiously in his notepad, finding solace in the world he created on paper.

Despite the challenges, Thomas was determined to build a new life. He enrolled in evening classes at a community college, his days a relentless cycle of work, study, and snatched moments of sleep. He started with basic courses—English, Math, and a design class that ignited his soul.

The classrooms were filled with people from all walks of life—immigrants learning English, single parents seeking a better future, dreamers like him, chasing a different destiny. He found a sense of camaraderie there, a shared understanding of the sacrifices required to learn and grow.

Some nights, he'd finish his shift at the hotel at 7 AM, grab a quick shower, and head straight to class, fueled by caffeine and sheer willpower. He'd sit in the back row, his eyes heavy but his mind ablaze with new ideas.

He excelled in his design classes, his sketches catching the eye of his professors, who encouraged him to pursue his talent. But he also knew that a stable income was essential. The hotel job, despite its drawbacks, provided that stability.

The days turned into months, each one a testament to his resilience. He learned to navigate the complexities of his dual existence—the demanding world of the hotel and the inspiring realm of design school. He was exhausted, often overwhelmed, but he was also filled with a growing sense of purpose. He was building himself, piece by piece, into the person he was meant to be.

And then, the day finally came.

He sat on the edge of his bed, holding the small orange pill bottle in his hand. Estrogen. His fingers shook. Tears welled up, unbidden. This wasn't just medicine—it was permission. A doorway.

He whispered the name he had chosen for herself. "Arora." The syllables were soft, radiant. Her name.

Becoming Arora wasn't easy. She faced slurs shouted on the street. She lost jobs after employers "reevaluated staffing needs." She was misgendered, mocked, and even once followed home. But she refused to shrink. With fierce determination, she enrolled in night classes, eventually getting into law school. By day, she worked. By night, she studied. She fought exhaustion, hunger, loneliness—but she kept going.

Because for the first time in her life, she was becoming real.

Across the city, Jasmin's path began differently—but no less brave.

On her eighteenth birthday, she didn't run. She stood her ground. After dinner, she asked her parents to sit down. Her voice quivered, but her hands didn't.

"I'm not your daughter," she said, each word like a stone in her throat. "I never was. I'm your son."

Her mother burst into tears, eyes wide with heartbreak and confusion. Her father just stared at her—*at him*—like he'd been punched in the chest.

But then, silence gave way to something rare: understanding.

"You are our child," her father said eventually, his voice cracking, "no matter what form your truth takes."

Ryan's mother held him tightly that night. She wept into his shoulder, whispering, "I just want you safe." And for the first time, Ryan believed safety and authenticity might coexist.

With his family behind him, Ryan transitioned with a kind of grace that surprised even him. His first testosterone shot left him dizzy but euphoric. Each physical change felt like a homecoming—his jawline sharpening, his voice lowering, the soft fuzz on his face growing with each passing week.

The first time he bought jeans and a fitted hoodie from the men's section, the cashier didn't even blink. That night, he stared at his reflection and smiled.

*There you are.*

He threw himself into building something new—not just a life, but a purpose. He launched a tech startup aimed at creating safe digital spaces for queer youth. He recruited other trans developers, gave jobs to those struggling to find acceptance elsewhere. His office was filled with pride flags, secondhand furniture, and *hope*.

Two people. Two lives, forged through fire.

Arora, with her quiet strength and fierce ambition, learning to speak for those silenced.

Ryan, with his vision and warmth, creating space for those who needed to *be*.

They didn't know each other yet. But the city had begun to move its pieces. A flyer tacked to a community center board. A chance encounter on a rainy night. A job application. A protest. A whisper of fate.
*Soon, they would meet.*

And when they did, everything would change.

# Chapter 3: A Fateful Encounter

It was a crisp autumn morning in New York City—the kind where golden leaves danced through the air like confetti and breath curled in soft wisps from the lips of early risers. The city pulsed with its usual rhythm: distant sirens, the hum of traffic, the hiss of espresso machines, and the comforting chatter of strangers blending into a familiar urban symphony.

Inside a tucked-away café in Midtown, nestled between a bookstore and a florist, Arora sat by the fogged-up window. Her espresso sat half-full on the table beside a stack of case files on her tablet. She wore a tailored black coat and soft woolen scarf, her hair tucked behind one ear. Her fingers scrolled through legal notes, but her mind kept drifting.

Another eviction case, she sighed inwardly, another trans teen kicked out by their family. It weighed on her, but she had learned to turn grief into fire. Her work was her weapon, and she wielded it with purpose.

Her office at the law firm was a world of polished wood and hushed conversations. She navigated it with a quiet determination, earning the respect of her colleagues with her sharp legal mind and unwavering dedication to her clients. But it wasn't always easy.

Sometimes, she'd catch the lingering stares, the hushed whispers after she left a room. Some of the older partners, set in their ways, still struggled with using her correct pronouns. She'd correct them gently but firmly, her voice calm but unwavering. She had a job to do, and she wouldn't let their ignorance derail her.

She found solace in the small victories: a hard-won settlement for a vulnerable client, a judge who recognized her expertise, the quiet satisfaction of knowing she was making a difference.
Outside, Ryan adjusted the strap of his backpack and pulled his hoodie tighter against the breeze. His phone buzzed in his pocket—an investor email, a calendar alert, a Slack ping. The world of tech never slept, but today, he needed caffeine more than answers.

His office was a stark contrast to Arora's: a vibrant, open-plan space filled with the buzz of creativity and the energy of young entrepreneurs. He thrived in the chaos, bouncing ideas off his team, fueled by passion and a seemingly endless supply of coffee.

But the pressure was immense. He was constantly pitching to investors, chasing deadlines, and putting out fires. He often worked late into the night, the glow of his laptop illuminating his face as he wrestled with lines of code and complex algorithms. He pushed open the café door.

The warm aroma of cinnamon, roasted beans, and fresh pastries enveloped him. He stepped inside—and paused.

There she was.

Sitting alone in the corner, framed by the golden morning light streaming through the window like a halo, was Arora. He didn't know her name. He didn't know her story. But something about her—a quiet intensity, the curve of her jaw, the steel in her posture—made the air feel different. He stood still, as if the city had hit pause.

Their eyes met.

Arora looked up, sensing the weight of his gaze. Their eyes locked—hers sharp and curious, his wide and momentarily unguarded. The moment stretched, soft and strange, before the bustle of the café snapped it back.

Ryan cleared his throat and moved to the counter, embarrassed at being caught staring. "Large black coffee," he mumbled to the barista, trying not to sneak another glance. But he couldn't help himself. As he turned to leave, his feet stopped of their own accord. He glanced again. She was still watching him.

On impulse—reckless, electric impulse—he stepped toward her table. "Excuse me," he said, trying to sound casual, "but… have we met before?" Arora tilted her head, intrigued. A slow, amused smile appeared on her lips. "I don't think so," she said, her voice smooth like velvet. "But New York is a small world."

Ryan chuckled, rubbing the back of his neck. "I guess it is." He hesitated, then extended a hand.

"I'm Ryan."

"Arora," she replied, shaking it.

Her grip was firm. Confident. He liked that.

There was a pause—a heartbeat, maybe two—before Arora gestured to the empty seat across from her. “You’re welcome to sit. If you’re not in a rush.” He blinked, surprised. Then smiled. “I’ve got a few minutes.”

Ryan slid into the chair, and just like that, the world outside the café blurred. They talked about the weather first, then favorite coffee orders, then the chaos of the city. She asked what he did. He told her about his startup—how he was trying to build something meaningful. She listened, really listened, and that shook him more than he expected.

He found himself drawn to her quiet strength, the way her eyes sparkled when she talked about her work, her passion for justice. He was used to the fast-paced, high-energy world of tech, but Arora's calm presence was a refreshing change.

When she mentioned her work as a lawyer, his brows rose in admiration. “That’s... amazing,” he said genuinely. “You’re helping people survive in a world that doesn’t make it easy.”

Arora’s lips curved again, but this time, it was softer. “I try.”

Their drinks grew cold. Time slipped through the cracks unnoticed. Outside, the leaves continued to fall, but inside, something had just begun to rise. A flicker of connection.

A bridge between two lives shaped by pain, carved by courage, and now—by possibility.

As the weeks passed, their professional relationship deepened. They collaborated on projects, their skills complementing each other perfectly. Ryan admired Arora's sharp legal mind, her ability to cut through complex issues with clarity and precision. Arora was impressed by Ryan's innovative thinking, his boundless energy, and his genuine desire to make a difference in the world.

Their late-night work sessions became a blend of business and personal connection. They'd share takeout and stories, their laughter echoing through the quiet office. Ryan would often find reasons to extend their meetings, lingering in Arora's office, asking "just one more question" even when the issue was resolved.

One evening, after a particularly long day, they found themselves alone in the office, the city lights twinkling outside the window. Ryan walked Arora to her car.

"Thanks for everything today," he said, his voice a little husky. "I don't know what I would have done without you."

Arora smiled, her eyes sparkling in the dim light. "You would have figured it out. You always do."
He hesitated, then took a step closer. "Maybe. But it's a lot better with you around."

A comfortable silence settled between them. The air crackled with unspoken feelings.

"Ryan," Arora said softly, breaking the silence.
"Yeah?"

"I... I've really enjoyed getting to know you."
He reached out and gently brushed a strand of hair from her cheek. "Me too, Arora. More than I can say."

Their eyes met, and the world seemed to shrink, focusing on the connection between them. He leaned in, his gaze searching hers, and then their lips met in a kiss that was both tender and electric. It was a kiss that spoke volumes, a culmination of weeks of shared moments, unspoken desires, and a growing affection that neither of them could deny.

# Chapter 4: Unraveling Bonds

New York City became their canvas—every coffee shop corner, every tree-lined path in Central Park, every streetlight-lit stroll through the Village painted with shared moments and quiet discoveries. Arora and Ryan weren't just falling in love; they were slowly learning to trust the world again, one heartbeat at a time.

What began as casual coffee meetups turned into routine, like breath and gravity. They wandered through bookstores and street fairs, debated politics over pad thai, and fell asleep on the phone while recounting stories of childhood they had once locked away. Each word exchanged was a thread, weaving them closer.

But even in love, healing isn't linear.

One cool October evening, the city bathed in amber and twilight, they walked hand in hand across the Brooklyn Bridge. The wind nipped at their jackets, and the hum of the city echoed beneath their feet.

Ryan paused mid-step, his fingers tightening slightly around Arora's. She turned to him, sensing something shifts.

"I used to come here a lot when I was a teenager," he said quietly, gazing out over the water. "Back when I felt… invisible. Like I could disappear into the skyline, and no one would notice."

Arora didn't speak—just moved a little closer, her warmth an anchor.

"I was fifteen the first time someone shoved me against a locker and called me a freak," he continued. "They said I was trying too hard to be a boy. Like it was something I could never really be. I started to believe them."

He paused; the memory still sharp after all these years. He remembered the smell of the locker, the cold metal against his back, the laughter echoing in the crowded hallway. He remembered the burning shame, the desperate desire to disappear.

"For years, I hated myself for not being what everyone expected. I hated my voice. My face. Even my walk."

He looked at her then, his eyes glossy beneath the bridge lights. “I didn’t think anyone would ever see me. Not like this.”

Arora’s voice was gentle, but steady. “I see you, Ryan. I always have.”

He smiled, but it trembled at the edges. “I’m still learning how to see myself.”

She reached up, brushing a wind-blown curl from his forehead. “That’s okay. I’m still learning, too.”

The bridge creaked beneath passing footsteps and cyclists. Around them, the world continued—lovers snapping selfies, tourists pointing at the skyline, joggers weaving through the crowd. But in their little pocket of the universe, time stood still.

Arora leaned on the railing, staring out into the darkness where the river met the sky. “I used to think I’d never be safe,” she said quietly. “That I’d spend my whole life fighting to exist. And some days… I still feel like I have to earn my right to take up space.”

She hesitated; the vulnerability clear in her voice. She remembered the countless nights she'd spent studying in dimly lit libraries, fueled by cheap coffee and the fear of failure. She remembered the sting of rejection letters from law firms, the subtle prejudice that hinted she wasn't quite the "right fit."

“Even now, even with you, I’m afraid. Of being hurt. Of not being enough. Of losing everything I’ve fought so hard to become.”

Ryan stepped beside her, slipping his hand into hers again. “We’re both scared,” he said. “But maybe that’s what makes this real.”

He thought about his own struggles—the sleepless nights spent coding, the constant pressure to prove himself in the cutthroat world of tech, the fear that his company, his dream, could crumble at any moment. He knew what it meant to fight for something, to build a life against the odds.

Their silence spoke volumes. And in it, they understood something profound: love wasn’t the end of their pain—it was the space where it could be witnessed, held, and slowly healed.

They walked the rest of the way in quiet, fingers entwined, shoulders brushing, hearts exposed. And though neither of them said it out loud, they both felt the same unspoken truth settling between them:

They were no longer alone.

# Chapter 5: Falling in Love

Their dinners became more frequent, slowly evolving into something more than just meals shared between colleagues. There was a new rhythm to their time together—unspoken, yet unmistakable. Arora found herself looking forward to Ryan's texts, the subtle way he remembered her coffee order, or how he always seemed to know when she needed a quiet evening instead of a bustling restaurant.

One evening, they met at a wine bar tucked away in the Lower East Side. It was raining gently outside, the city blurred in gold reflections on wet pavement. They sat near the window, sharing a bottle of red and talking long after their plates were cleared.

The conversation flowed effortlessly, moving from lighthearted banter to deeper, more intimate Sharing their dreams, their fears, and their vulnerabilities. With each passing moment, their connection deepened, drawing them closer.

After a pause in conversation, Arora leaned back, swirling her wine and watching the raindrops trickle down the glass. "You know," she said softly, "I always wondered what would've happened if we had stayed together back then."

Ryan looked at her, thoughtful. "I think about it too. But we were different people then—so caught up in proving ourselves."

She nodded slowly. "I was so afraid of failing, of not meeting expectations. I pushed people away… even you."

He reached across the table, his fingers brushing hers before gently holding her hand. "I wasn't any better. I was too focused on my goals to realize what I was losing."

Their hands lingered, the warmth of their touch a silent language. In that moment, the years that had separated them seemed to melt away, replaced by a sense of belonging.

A silence settled between them—not heavy, not uncomfortable, but honest. It was the silence of two people finally letting go of the weight they'd carried for too long. They didn't need to fill it. The understanding between them said more than words ever could.

Over the weeks that followed, their conversations grew deeper. They shared the parts of themselves usually hidden away—the losses, the fears, the vulnerable truths no one else had touched.

One night, curled up on Ryan's couch with a blanket wrapped around her shoulders and the soft glow of the city flickering through the window, Arora confessed, "I lost a big case once. Early in my career. It felt like the end of everything I'd worked for. I thought I wasn't good enough. But it taught me resilience. Taught me to rebuild myself from the ground up."

Her voice was thick with emotion as she recounted the grueling trial, the sleepless nights spent poring over documents, and the crushing disappointment of the verdict. Ryan listened intently, his gaze filled with empathy and admiration for her strength.

Ryan, seated beside her, reached for her hand. "I know that feeling. I pitched my idea to twelve investors before one finally said yes. Each 'no' felt personal. Like maybe I didn't belong. But I kept going. And somehow… it all worked out."

He shared his own stories of struggle and perseverance, the setbacks and failures that had threatened to derail his dreams. Through their shared vulnerabilities, a deeper intimacy blossomed between them.

Their stories wove together, their scars becoming shared maps of survival. The emotional armor they had once worn so tightly began to fall away, piece by piece.

Arora found herself laughing more—deep, unguarded laughter that surprised even her. Ryan caught himself staring at her when she wasn't looking, heart beating a little faster every time she brushed a strand of hair behind her ear or said his name in that warm, grounding voice.

Their connection deepened, transcending the professional realm. One evening, as they walked home from dinner, the air was cool, and the city had quieted. They moved slowly, their steps in sync, the world around them fading.

The restaurant had been cozy and intimate, the candlelight casting a soft glow on their faces. As they strolled through the city streets, hand in hand, they talked about their dreams for the future, their passions, and their shared desire to make a difference in the world.

Then Ryan stopped. He turned to her, his eyes searching hers with a tenderness that made her breath catch.

"Arora," he said quietly, "I don't want to keep wondering about 'what ifs' anymore. I want to try—really try—with you."

His voice was filled with a raw honesty, a vulnerability that mirrored her own. In that moment, all the walls she had built around her heart crumbled, replaced by a wave of hope.

She looked at him for a long moment. Then, for the first time in years, she let the walls fall completely. Her voice was almost a whisper. "Neither do I."

He cupped her face, his thumb brushing her cheek, and she closed her eyes, leaning into the warmth of his touch. When their lips met, it wasn't rushed or dramatic—it was soft, certain, and full of promise. A kiss born not just of passion, but of understanding.

The world around them faded away as they lost themselves in the intimacy of the moment. It was a kiss that sealed their connection.

In that moment, they knew.

The past had shaped them, yes—but it no longer defined them.

What mattered now was the present—and the undeniable truth that they had found their way back to each other.

And this time, they weren't letting go.

As their relationship deepened, they also faced new challenges in their professional lives. Arora's unwavering commitment to justice often put her at odds with powerful figures, leading to threats and intimidation. She found herself caught in a web of ethical dilemmas, where doing the right thing came at a great personal cost.

Meanwhile, Ryan's tech company faced a series of setbacks. A rival company launched a smear campaign, questioning his integrity and the viability of his product. Investors grew skittish, and he faced the daunting prospect of losing everything he had worked for.

These external pressures tested their bond, pushing them to rely on each other for support and strength.

# Chapter 6: Challenges and Drama

Just as their relationship solidified, challenges arose. Arora faced workplace discrimination—a senior partner undermining her authority, questioning her abilities despite her track record. She tried to brush it off, but Ryan saw the toll it took on her.

"It's not fair," he said one evening as they sat on his couch. "You work harder than anyone."
"It's the way things are," she murmured. "But I won't let it break me."

Things became even more complicated when past bullies resurfaced—old rivals from law school attempting to discredit her, former competitors of Ryan trying to sabotage his company.

Amidst the chaos, Ryan's parents embraced Arora with open arms, welcoming her as part of their family. But Arora's parents weren't as accepting. They disapproved of her relationship, fearing it would disrupt tradition and expectations.

"I love them, but I can't keep living for their approval," Arora confided in Ryan. "I need to make my own choices."

And then, the ultimate test came—a legal battle that threatened Ryan's company. A competitor accused him of intellectual property theft, and the lawsuit could destroy everything he built. Without hesitation, Arora took on the case, standing by his side as his fiercest advocate.

During the intense courtroom battle, Arora's brilliance shone. She dismantled every false accusation, proving Ryan's innocence. Through the long hours and sleepless nights, their bond grew even stronger.

When the final verdict was announced in Ryan's Favor, he turned to her, gratitude and love overflowing in his eyes. "I don't know what I would've done without you."

"You don't have to," she whispered, taking his hand. "We're in this together."

Through trials and triumphs, their love not only survived—it thrived, proving that no challenge was too great when they stood together.

Ryan and Arora overcame every challenge life threw at them, proving that love transcends all boundaries. But the final road to happiness was not without its trials.

The weeks following Ryan's court victory were tumultuous. Arora's firm, despite her success, faced internal backlash. Some senior partners saw her as a liability for taking on such a high-profile case with personal ties. Whispers circulated about her judgment, questioning if she had let love cloud her professional ethics.

One afternoon, Arora was called into a board meeting. The atmosphere was tense.

"We acknowledge your contribution to the firm," one of the partners said, his tone laced with condescension. "But we cannot ignore the… complications your recent case has brought."

Arora stiffened. "Complications?"

"Clients have raised concerns about favoritism. You understand how this affects our reputation."

Arora's jaw clenched. She had poured everything into this firm, yet they questioned her integrity the moment she chose to fight for something personal.

"Are you asking me to step down?" she asked, her voice calm but edged with steel.

"We're suggesting a voluntary sabbatical. Time to let things cool down."

She stood, straightening her blazer. "I don't need time. I need a firm that values me. Consider this my resignation."

With that, she walked out, leaving behind years of dedication for the uncertain—but exhilarating—freedom of a new beginning.

Meanwhile, Ryan faced his own battle. Though he had won the lawsuit, his competitor hadn't given up. Rumors of corporate espionage plagued his company, investors grew wary, and one by one, funding deals started slipping away.

One night, he sat in his office, staring at the financial reports. Arora walked in, carrying takeout.

"You look like you're trying to solve quantum physics," she teased, setting the food down.

Ryan sighed. "It's bad, Arora. Investors are backing out. I thought winning the case would be the end of it, but it's just the beginning of another war."

She sat beside him. "Then we fight again."

He looked at her, admiration shining in his eyes. “You just walked away from your firm. You should be focusing on yourself, not my mess.”

Arora took his hand. “Your fight is my fight now. We’re in this together, remember?”

Ryan exhaled, leaning his forehead against hers. “I don’t deserve you.”
She smiled. “You absolutely do.”

Determined not to let his company fall apart, Ryan met with a group of independent investors, this time presenting his vision not just as a business plan but as a mission fueled by resilience. Arora stood by his side, offering legal and strategic counsel, ensuring every move was airtight.

Slowly, the tides turned. One investor signed on. Then another. Soon, Ryan’s company was back on stable ground, stronger than before. And standing at the heart of it all was Arora—his partner in every sense of the word.

But one battle remained: Arora's parents.

They still refused to acknowledge her relationship with Ryan. Every call with them ended in disappointment, their voices filled with disapproval.

"Son, he is a good man, but this is not the life we wanted for you," her mother pleaded one evening.

Arora's heart ached. "This is my life, Mom. And I am happy."

Her father remained silent; his silence heavicr than any words of rejection.

It wasn't until weeks later, when Arora's mother unexpectedly visited her apartment, that things changed. She saw the framed photos of Arora and Ryan, the way they fit into each other's world so seamlessly.

"Tell me honestly," her mother said, her voice soft. "Does he make you happy?"

Arora's eyes welled up. "Yes, Maa. More than anything."
Her mother sighed, reaching for her hand. "Then maybe… we need to learn to be happy for you."

It was a start. A step toward acceptance.

With their love stronger than ever, Ryan and Arora decided to build a future together. As they stood on the rooftop of their apartment, looking at the city lights, Ryan pulled out a small velvet box.

Arora gasped. “Ryan…”

“I don’t need anything else in this life except you,” he said, kneeling before her. “Will you marry me?”

Tears slipped down her cheeks as she nodded. “Yes. A thousand times yes.”

He slipped the ring onto her finger, and as they kissed, the city below seemed to disappear, leaving only them, bound by love, unbreakable.
And so, their journey continued—proving that true love isn’t just about finding each other, but about fighting for each other, against all odds.

# Chapter 7: Happy Ending

The wedding was only days away, but Arora's heart was a whirlwind of emotions. Despite everything they had conquered, the one shadow that lingered was the silence from her father.

One evening, she stood by the window, staring at the city lights, the wedding invitation resting in her hand. Ryan came up behind her, wrapping his arms gently around her waist.

"You're thinking about them again," he said softly.

She nodded, unable to speak. "I know they love me, but I still feel like I'm losing them."

"You're not," he whispered. "Sometimes love just takes longer to understand."

Just then, the doorbell rang.

Arora's heart skipped a beat. She wasn't expecting anyone.
When she opened the door, she froze.

Her mother stood there, teary-eyed, with a jasmine garland in her hand—one that used to hang at their family altar. Behind her, her father stood tall, holding an envelope, his jaw set tight but his eyes shimmering.

“Can we come in?” her mother asked softly.

Arora stepped aside, wordless, as they entered. Her father looked around the apartment—at the framed photos of her and Ryan, the books stacked on the coffee table, the soft scent of lavender in the air. A home, lived in. Loved.
He handed her the envelope. She opened it with trembling fingers.

Inside was a letter. It read:

***"Mydearestdaughter,***
***When you were born, I imagined the life you would have. I held dreams for you—many shaped by the world I knew. But I forgot to leave space for the dreams you would shape for yourself.***

***I was wrong to measure your choices against tradition. What I should have seen was the courage it took to live truthfully. To love truthfully.***

***And so, I come to you not with judgment, but with a humble heart. If you will have us, we would be honoured to stand by you on your wedding day.***

Arora's tears spilled freely now. She reached for her father, and to her surprise, he didn't just allow the embrace—he pulled her into it.
Ryan watched from a distance; eyes misty, overwhelmed by the grace of the moment.

## Wedding Day

The sun rose on a perfect spring morning. The garden venue bloomed with soft florals, lanterns swaying gently in the breeze. Rows of chairs were filled with guests—colleagues, friends, family—each holding their breath for the ceremony to begin.

Ryan stood beneath the mandap, heart pounding. He wore a cream sherwani with a maroon stole draped across his shoulder, his eyes searching for her.

And then—she appeared.

Arora walked down the aisle in a rich maroon sari embroidered with gold. Her mother held one hand. Her father held the other. Their faces beamed with pride, no longer burdened by uncertainty.

Ryan's breath caught.

She looked like everything he'd ever hoped for and more—strength and softness wrapped into one.
As Arora reached him, her parents gently placed her hands in his.

"Take care of our daughter," her father whispered.

"I will," Ryan replied, voice thick with emotion.

**Vows Beneath the Sky**

The priest began the rituals. Sacred chants echoed under the canopy of trees.

Ryan turned to her, his eyes never leaving hers.

"I choose you," he said, voice trembling. "In success, in failure. In every beginning and every storm. You are my home."

Arora's voice was steady, even as her eyes shone with tears. "And I choose you. Through judgment and acceptance. In all your chaos and calm. You are my truth."

When they kissed, the crowd erupted in applause—but for them, the world narrowed to just this moment.

Two people. One bond. Unshakable.

## Later That Night

As guests departed and the lanterns flickered in the wind, Ryan and Arora stood on the rooftop of their apartment, barefoot, wrapped in one shawl, holding glasses of sparkling water.
"Did that really just happen?" Arora laughed breathlessly.
Ryan smiled, brushing a curl behind her ear. "You're my wife now."

She grinned. "And you're stuck with me forever."

He grew quiet, looking out over the city. "Arora, do you ever think about how close we came to missing this?"

She nodded. "All the time."

"But we didn't," he said. "We fought. We bled. We broke. And still—here we are."

Arora looked up at him, heart full. "Because we chose each other."

He kissed her again, softer this time, as the wind whispered around them, carrying the scent of jasmine and the laughter of the day.

Below them, the city moved on—cars honked, sirens wailed, life spun forward. But up here, on their little rooftop world, time slowed. The chaos of life faded.

Only love remained—wounded, tested, and finally… victorious.

www.ingramcontent.com/pod-product-compliance
Lightning Source LLC
Chambersburg PA
CBHW062113160726
48282CB00026B/789
* 9 7 8 9 3 3 4 2 8 2 5 5 9 *